Trickster and
the Fainting Birds

Trickster and the Fainting Birds

Told by Howard Norman

Illustrated by Tom Pohrt

GULLIVER BOOKS

HARCOURT BRACE & COMPANY

San Diego   New York   London

Requests for permission to make copies of any part of the work should be mailed to:
Permissions Department, Harcourt Brace & Company, 6277 Sea Harbor Drive,
Orlando, Florida 32887-6777.

Gulliver Books is a registered trademark of Harcourt Brace & Company.

Library of Congress Cataloging-in-Publication Data
Norman, Howard A.
Trickster and the fainting birds/told by Howard Norman;
illustrated by Tom Pohrt.
p.   cm.
"Gulliver Books."
Includes bibliographical references.
Summary: A collection of seven Cree and Chippewa trickster tales.
ISBN 0-15-200888-8
1. Cree Indians—Folklore.   2. Ojibwa Indians—Folklore.   3. Trickster—Juvenile literature.
[1. Cree Indians—Folklore.   2. Ojibwa Indians—Folklore.   3. Indians of North America—
Folklore.   4. Trickster.]   I. Pohrt, Tom, ill.   II. Title.
E99.C9N67   1999
398.2'089973—dc21   97-9457

First edition
F E D C B A

Printed in Singapore

The illustrations in this book were done in pen, ink, and watercolor
on vintage T. H. Saunders paper.
The display type was set in Alcoholica.
The text type was set in Berkeley Book.
Color separations by United Graphic Pte. Ltd., Singapore
Printed and bound by Tien Wah Press, Singapore
This book was printed on totally chlorine-free Nymolla Matte Art paper.
Production supervision by Stanley Redfern and Pascha Gerlinger
Designed by Kaelin Chappell

For my daughter, Emma
For Jaime de Angulo
                    —H. N.

For Madeleine and Annie
                    —T. P.

Contents

Introduction:
Endless Wandering, Endless Mischief   ix

Trickster and the Best Hermit   *1*

Trickster and the Shut-Eye Dancers   *13*

Trickster Tells Whiskey Jack the Truth   *29*

Trickster and the Walking Contest   *39*

Trickster and the Clacking Sleeves   *49*

Trickster and the Night-Tailed Weasels   *61*

Trickster and the Fainting Birds   *71*

Story Notes   81

Endless Wandering, Endless Mischief

The third story in this collection, "Trickster Tells Whiskey Jack the Truth," was the first Trickster tale I ever wrote down. I heard it in the late spring of 1974 from an East Cree man named Albert Sandy, near Family Lake in northern Manitoba, Canada, a region of spruce, white birch, and pine trees with lakes and rivers abounding. Albert was, I would guess, about fifty-five years old. He was a native speaker of Cree, which is part of the Algonquian family of languages spoken from the prairie of Alberta province all the way to the Labrador coast. Trickster stories have been told by Algonquian peoples for centuries. Albert's name for Trickster was *Wistchahik*, but in other Cree communities I have heard it as *Wesucechak*, *Wichikapache*, or other close variations on these pronunciations. In this book, I simply call him *Trickster*, because it is the most generally recognized usage in English.

That spring I was working my way from Eskimo Point and Churchill, Manitoba, southward through any number of Cree villages and fishing camps. When I met Albert Sandy, he invited me to stay with him and his cousin John Rains for a few weeks.

One cold, drizzly morning on our way back from a fishing excursion, Albert stopped his pickup truck on an abandoned logging road and said, "Let's have some coffee and something to eat." He reached into his wicker creel, took out some sandwiches, and handed them around. John opened a thermos of coffee. Albert lowered the driver's-side window, and as he took a few puffs on a cigarette, all of a sudden a bird known as Whiskey Jack (and also called a Camp Robber because it likes to hang around fishing and hunting camps begging and darting in for scraps of food) landed on the broken side-view mirror. Not a moment had passed when Whiskey Jack let loose a call like a rusty pump handle, followed by a comical and highly annoying concert of squawks, hiccups, chortles, clicks, and a strange sound similar to that made by a chattering teeth windup toy. What a bold pest! "Don't toss it even a crust," Albert warned me. He and John both laughed. "Because then you'll have Whiskey Jack riding with us all day!" Albert honked the truck's horn, and Whiskey Jack flitted off, only to land on the tailgate. Albert took a sip of coffee, then said, "Whiskey Jack was a complainer—a complaint bird!"

Then out tumbled a story in which Wistchahik/Trickster tried to teach stubborn Whiskey Jack a few ways to get along better in the world. The story lasted maybe ten minutes. However, with its slapstick humor and animals talking with each other (Albert did a splendid imitation of Whiskey Jack's voices), the story conveyed an overall feeling of timelessness. And though hearing Albert's story was my introduction to Wistchahik and Whiskey Jack, it felt like a reunion with old friends. I did not want to leave their world. But, alas, Albert ended by saying, "That's what happened." John simply nodded and finished his sandwich. Finally, Albert switched on the ignition, Whiskey Jack flew from the truck, and off we went down the road.

The very next day I ventured to ask Albert if he might tell me the story again. "I'll tell it, sure," he said. "But I might remember something else that happened, and put that in." So, for each of the next ten days, Albert and I spent time together, sitting outside or in a tent. I would open my spiral notebook. Albert would pour a ton of sugar into his black coffee. "Now, this is about Whiskey Jack," he would begin. Or, "Wistchahik was out walking," or, "Whiskey Jack was complaining about his feathers." And we were off and running.

Truth be told, the pace of our work together was more like walking in slow motion. Albert had decided that as long as we were sitting down together, he might as well offer me language lessons. I welcomed this, and Albert proved to be immeasurably patient with my embarrassingly meager knowledge of Cree vocabulary. First Albert would tell the story in his native tongue, then require me to repeat certain phrases, all the while chuckling at my awkward pronunciations. Then he would say, "Now, write this down as best you can," and tell me the story in English as he had that first time in the truck, with a few Cree and French words tossed in. From the outset, Albert saw that my initial talent for the Cree language was laughable. Nonetheless, we stubborned along. He worked through the story again and again, much the way a kindergarten teacher might instruct a five-year-old to read: "See Jane run. See Dick run." In the end, I wrote down five quite similar versions of "Trickster Tells Whiskey Jack the Truth." I remember Albert saying, "As a boy, I mostly heard Wistchahik stories in wintertime. After supper, eh? A drum was passed around . . . and then the stories. Wistchahik came right inside the house. Came right on in."

One form or another of Trickster thrives in almost every tribal region of the world, whether it be among the Aboriginal peoples of Australia, the Chukchee of the Siberian tundra, or the Makiritare Indians of the Orinoco River rain forest in Venezuela. Throughout North America, the most popular Tricksters are Raven and Coyote, but there are also mink, spider, and blue jay Tricksters, and a wide variety of other animal Tricksters. Wistchahik/Trickster is in the near-human category, but in Algonquian oral tradition you will not hear an actual physical description of him. What you will get is an absolutely vivid description of what he *turns into,* whether it be animal or human being. But shape-shifting is scarcely the only behavior Trickster entertains us with. As Richard Erdoes and Alfonso Ortiz write in their splendid *American Indian Trickster Tales,* "It's Trickster who provides the real spark in the action—always hungry for another meal swiped from someone else's kitchen, always ready to lure someone else's wife into bed, always trying to get something for nothing, getting caught in the act, never acting remorseful."

In each and every story Trickster is a master craftsman of mischief, using all the natural materials at hand—cunning, bravery, cowardice, greed, lust, curiosity, wit, vanity—to shake things up, to set the world slightly askew. Human beings and animals alike have to muster every ounce of strength, have to tap deep into their imaginations and wisdom, to fight back. That is the ancient give-and-take of Trickster stories. In the meantime, there is never a dull moment. There might be lots of bickering, insults, bragging. Maybe someone dies, maybe someone gets married. Anything can happen, really. One thing is for certain: When Trickster is in the neighborhood, topsy-turvy predicaments arise, one after the next. Trickster might set up a bevy of small problems to be solved—or he might foist one big problem on a village. And like a cloudburst, a mosquito flown into your ear, or any ambush of Nature, Trickster demands immediate attention: He likes to be at the center of things. Clown, thief, magician, lover, liar, doctor, raconteur—Trickster has quite a few mythological vocations. Charming one minute, horribly selfish the next, Trickster has been—and always will be— a bundle of contradictions.

Now and then Trickster might try out life as a human being, or a crow, or a bear—he might even raise children—but, eventually, he will turn back into Trickster again. Like a magic hermit, he is destined to live outside of civilization, because Trickster's ultimate fate is to wander. Endless, endless wandering. Endless troublemaking. These have gone on for hundreds of years, and there is no end to it in sight! We can be grateful for this, because as Trickster meanders the North, stories follow in his footsteps. "We tell about Wistchahik," Albert Sandy once remarked, "because he's always been around."

I worked with the other five Cree Indian men whose stories grace this book in pretty much the same way as I did with Albert Sandy. In the "story notes" section in back, I write about each collaboration in some detail.

I have been honored to witness myriad tellings of Trickster stories throughout the North. I have notebooks full of fragments, as well as complete stories. I have admired and learned much from the prominent studies of Algonquian oral literature. Linguist Robert Brightman's *Acaōo ohk iwina and Acim owina: Traditional Narratives of the Rock Cree Indians,* a monograph from the Canadian Museum of Civilization, for example, offers an exemplary collection of transliterated Trickster stories, and is a definitive ethnographic, linguistic, historical portrait of Rock Cree oral tradition in general. Of course, there are many outstanding arguments and questions about translation from one language to another, let alone from a spoken language to a written one. How authentic can a translation truly be? How much of the original sights, sounds, tastes, and smells of age-old folktales can be "brought over" into a different language? These are vital questions that I cannot answer. As for my small part in presenting *Trickster and the Fainting Birds* to an English-speaking audience, I have tried to construct a language that evokes both the *spoken* and the *written* word. My model for this comes not from linguistic or ethnographic theory, but from a mimeographed thirty-one page collection, *Stories Told by Grandparents,* given to me by a teenager near the Pelican Narrows Cree community in Saskatchewan. To me, this little booklet, with its type-ribbon smudges, spelling errors, and other informalities, is a profound example of the spirit of survival of Cree literature. Each brief tale (and some were two-sentence anecdotes) fairly leaped off the page! The writing (perhaps it was translation; this was not mentioned) was sophisticated and spontaneous, and precisely because of that the booklet became an inspiration while composing *Trickster and the Fainting Birds.*

My greatest hope is that you will find Trickster a great travel companion, whose outlandish antics nurture your imagination and make you laugh deep in your heart. I hope, too, that this book becomes like a hand-me-down suitcase, whose contents are ever-surprising, each time you open it. Why? Because Trickster stories are a celebration of life. But remember, Trickster has practiced being alone for a long, long, *long* time. So, be like the crows in "Trickster and the Best Hermit"—when Trickster shouts, "Get out of here!" . . . invite him along.

Howard Norman
East Calais, Vermont

Trickster and
the Fainting Birds

Trickster and the Best Hermit

Trickster stood in a snowy field
between stretches of spruce-tree forest.
Waving his arms, stomping his feet,
he scattered off a flock of crows.
"Go away!" he shouted.
"Get out of here!
Leave me alone!"

The crows settled in a spruce tree at the edge of the forest.

"Well, what do you think?" one crow said.
This crow spoke in a cough-voice—*cuff, cuff, cuff*—
which is just one of many voices used by crows.
"What do you think?"

Another crow said, "Surely Trickster is practicing to be alone!"
This crow spoke in harsh sighs and chortles—
uhh ccchhhttt, uhh ccchhhttt, chrrrrrrttttt—
which, of course, is yet another crow voice.

"Yes, he needs to be the best at everything, doesn't he?"
a third crow said with sudden gusts of rain-wind in its voice—
ssshoooo, wishoooo, shooo—
then clicks—*tttkkk ttkk catik, catik, catik.*
When crows get excited about something,
they use a lot of different voices to talk it over.

"The best at everything!
The best at everything!
The best at everything!"
all the crows sang out.
And the snowy field echoed with crow laughter.

"Maybe we should take Trickster over to see Hermit!"
a crow said.
"Yes, there will be a lesson in that," another crow said.
All the crows loudly agreed.

They flew from the tree and landed close to Trickster.
"Listen, Big Brother,"—
for that is what all the animals called him—
"we know who is best at being alone," a crow said.

Trickster could talk with crows.
Trickster spoke every animal language in the North.
"Why, thank you, Little Brothers," Trickster said.
"You crows are very smart to see that it is I, Trickster,
who can outmatch anyone at being alone!"

"No, no, no!" the crows shouted all at once.
"We meant Hermit!"

Trickster got angry.

He just managed to say, "You are wrong about that—!"
when two, three, four, five,
finally six more flocks of crows arrived!

Now there were hundreds of crows in the snowy field.
Trickster was surrounded by crows.
What's more, Trickster began to behave in a way
he never had before.
He hopped sideways, flapping his arms,
but he wasn't flying yet.
No, the crows hadn't used their full magic
to turn him into a flying crow, not just yet.

Then Trickster sprouted crows' feet!
No beak yet. No full-feathered black wings yet.

Now, Trickster had very powerful magic himself,
and he could turn into most anything he wanted.
But this time the magic of hundreds of crows was at work!
Crows were turning *Trickster* into a crow!

"Listen, Big Brother," one crow said,
"we're going over to see Hermit.
That's why so many of us are here.
A visit to Hermit is a rare, rare thing,
a once-in-a-lifetime thing,
and we're going to take you along!
Hermit lives in a place secret to everyone but us crows.
It's a faraway place,
a hidden place,
a lonely place,
at the edge of the world.
In fact, come to think of it,
maybe it's too lonely a place for you.
Maybe we should leave you behind!"

"Take me there!" Trickster said.
"And I'll have a match with this Hermit
to see who is best at being alone!"

"Very well," a crow said.

Every crow clacked its beak
and rustled its wings
and let loose with a deafening *Caw! Caw! Caw!*
Every last crow aimed its magic at Trickster!
The sound was so loud
Trickster clamped his black wings over his ears. . . .
The magic had worked and Trickster was now a crow.

The crows lifted from the ground
and started to fly over the trees,
and Trickster flew with them.

Up in the sky, Trickster looked down.
He saw the tops of trees.
He saw frozen rivers.
He saw a wolverine loping over a frozen lake.
He saw snow
and trees
and endless frozen lakes and ponds
with no wolverines loping over them.

They flew over a wide stretch of spruce trees,
and where the trees ended there was a shack.
Every crow landed.

Once on the ground,
the crows aimed their magic at Trickster again
and turned him back to his old self.

"Well," said a crow, "we'll be on our way now."
"But we just got here!" Trickster said.
"A quick visit is the best visit when it comes to hermits,"
another crow said.

"Well, do what you please," said Trickster.
"As for me, I'm waiting until Hermit shows himself.
Then I'll challenge him to a match.
We'll find out who wants to be alone more,
him or me!"

"Good luck, then," a few crows said.

The crows flew away.
It was very quiet in the snowy field
in front of Hermit's shack.

But Trickster did not have to wait long.

The door opened;
a voice from inside the shack said,
"What do you want here?"

Now, Trickster was good at lying.
In fact he might really have been the *best* liar in all the North.

And so he lied to Hermit.
"I've brought you a wife!" Trickster shouted.

"I already have a wife!" Hermit said.
With that, Hermit groaned and slammed the door,
without ever being seen!

That is something a hermit is good at.
The sound of a door slamming is one hermit voice.

Echo from the hermit's door.
Thick snow on the ground.
No crows anywhere to be seen.

Suddenly Trickster desperately missed his companions,
the crows.

Trickster hid among the trees.
He sat down.
He waited. He waited a long time.
He watched the shack. At first he heard nothing.
Finally some sounds came from inside the shack.

To hear better, Trickster snuck up
and pressed his ear to the shack.
He listened hard.
Trickster heard an otter slide down a snowbank—*Ssssshwooosh!*
Then another—*Sssshwooosh!*
Trickster knew the sound of sliding otters;
he had heard it many times,
but never coming from inside a shack!

Then he heard the sound of otters crunching down on fish.

Then he heard some bear grunts,
then a bear snapping twigs with its feet.

Otter sounds in there!
Bear sounds in there!

Hermit surely has powerful magic, thought Trickster,
to fit an otter snow slide inside his shack!

He listened some more.
He heard an otter say, "Good-bye.
We will tell your wife you are on your way to visit her."
He heard the otters scamper off over hard-packed, crusty snow.

He heard the bear sprawl on the ground,
grunting, yawning, as bears do.

And then Trickster knew:
Hermit was a bear!

Trickster hightailed it back to the trees.
He crouched out of sight.
He waited.

And sure enough, Hermit finally opened the door
and stepped out.

But much to Trickster's surprise,
Hermit was now a human being!

Trickster was learning many things about Hermit!
He learned that Hermit was a bear
who could turn into a human being,
and back into a bear again.

Carrying an otter-skin sack, Hermit set out into the forest.
Trickster followed along behind.
Trickster followed Hermit a long way.

Finally Hermit came to a clearing.
He reached into the otter-skin bag.
He took out some food.
Trickster had a keen sense of smell;
he smelled berries, honey,
sap-drenched bark—summer foods!
Hermit set the food on the ground.
Then Hermit backed away a few steps
and stood staring at the trees.

Hermit and Trickster waited all day.

Just at dusk Hermit's wife—a bear—
appeared at the edge of the forest.
"Hello, Husband," she said.
She ate the food.
Then she walked right up to Hermit, licked his face,
and said, "Good-bye, Husband."
"Good-bye, Wife," Hermit said.

Trickster watched their hellos and good-byes from hiding.
He watched the she-bear amble back into the forest.

Hermit set out for his shack.
Trickster followed him again.

At the end of dusk, just a haze of light in the sky,
Hermit reached his shack.
Suddenly he spun around,
waved his arms,
stomped his feet,
charged a few short steps toward Trickster,
and shouted, "Go away!"

Trickster stumbled backward
and did not stop until he was deep amongst the trees.
Then he stopped to look at Hermit's shack
one last time.

Hermit alone as a bear.
Hermit alone as a human being.

Trickster knew he could not match that loneliness.
He would have to settle for being second-best.
It was a tough lesson for Trickster to learn,
but he learned it.

Trickster walked and walked and walked . . .
all night long.
Just as it grew light on the horizon,
a single crow landed next to Trickster.
They traveled together across a snowy field.

Trickster and the Shut-Eye Dancers

Trickster and Fox crouched in dry reeds
at the edge of a marsh.
They were looking at ducks.
They had been watching ducks all morning.

"Remember, Fox," said Trickster, "be patient."
But suddenly Fox leaped from the reeds—
and the ducks flew off.

"Those ducks got the better of you!" Trickster said.
"Last time, geese got the better of you.
Before that, grebes got the better of you.
All the waterbirds get the better of you.
You can't just leap out at waterbirds.
You have to think up a better plan."

When the ducks landed again far across the marsh,
a loon was with them.

Trickster and Fox spent a hungry morning
moving through edge reeds, trying to sneak up on ducks.

That afternoon, when the ducks were drifting lazily in the sun,
some asleep,
some preening,
some bickering,
Trickster and Fox got closer.

"That loon is guarding the ducks," Trickster said.
"Now, Fox, notice there's no breeze.
So whatever you do,
don't rattle these reeds as if there is a breeze—
the ducks will startle up and fly off again."

Just then a marsh mosquito bothered Fox's face
and he swatted at it.
Doing so, he rattled the reeds.
"No breeze," the loon cried out,
"yet the reeds are moving!"
And all the ducks flew off.

"They're wise to us," Fox said.
"Let's just cook up some of these reeds.
Let's cook up some bark,
or maybe make a broth
of reeds, bark, and some duck feathers.
What do you say? I'm starving!"

"No," said Trickster. "I have a plan."

All during that dusk,
then all night long,
then much of the morning as Fox slept,
Trickster wove a dance lodge out of reeds.
He was a skillful weaver.
He did a fine job of it.
The lodge was big enough to hold a lot of waterbird dancers,
plus it had a strong door latch.
When Trickster finished the dance lodge,
he pulled Fox's tail and said, "Get awake! Get awake!"

They hid in the reeds looking at ducks.

"When you look long enough at ducks," Trickster said,
"it makes you hungry for ducks.
There's little else you need to know
on such a morning as this."

"I know it all right," Fox said.
"I'm looking at ducks—I'm hungry!"

Trickster took out his carry-sack made of moose hide,
and he said to Fox, "Dig up some clumps of moss."

Fox brought clumps of moss to Trickster,
who packed the moss into his carry-sack.

"Slowly now," Trickster said,
"we'll step right out into the open—
we'll just show ourselves!
And when the ducks and that loon get a big eyeful of us,
you press your face to the opening of this carry-sack
and shout into it."

"What do I shout?" said Fox.
"Just shout, 'I'm hungry for ducks!'" said Trickster.
"All right," said Fox.

Trickster and Fox sloshed out from the reeds—
and the loon hollered, "Watch out! Watch out!"

A few ducks flew off—
but when Fox shouted into the carry-sack,
most of the ducks just became curious.

"Hey, Big Brother, what's Fox shouting into that carry-sack?"
one duck said. "We can't make out what he's saying.
What's in the carry-sack, anyway?"

Trickster snatched the carry-sack away from Fox
and quickly tied it shut.

The ducks drifted closer—
the loon zigzagged between Trickster and the ducks,
muttering, "Be careful now. Be careful now."

"Tell us what's in the sack!" a duck said.

"It's our songs," said Trickster.
"Our best, most powerful songs."

"Oh, can we hear them?" many ducks asked at once.

"Ducks and Loon—dear friends," said Trickster,
"*of course* you can hear these songs!
I've built a special dance lodge.
Let's go there. You'll like it.
There's plenty of room to move around and dance.
It's a lodge woven of reeds from your very own marsh.
You'll feel right at home."

"I only like to dance at night
out in the middle of a lake," Loon said.

"Why not stay here, then?" said Trickster.
"After the dancing, the ducks will come back
and drift lazily with you
and tell you all about how well they danced."

"No, I'll come along," Loon said.
"But I won't dance.
I don't dance up close to anybody, except another loon.
I don't dance in lodges.
I only dance out in the middle of a lake.
At night or sometimes at dawn or dusk."

"Let's go, then," Trickster said.
The ducks and loon followed Trickster and Fox to the lodge.

When they got to the lodge Loon said,
"How come the door latch is on the outside of the door?
What if the ducks want to leave on their own?"

"That must've been a mistake," said Trickster.
"Just tear the latch off the door—go ahead, tear it off.
Then you can stay outside and keep watch while we dance."

"Fine with me," said Loon.

Loon pulled the latch off with his beak.
The latch was made of tightly woven reeds
and it cut Loon's mouth, but Loon didn't mind.

"The latch is gone," Loon said. "I'll guard the lodge now."

"I'm sure the ducks will feel safer knowing that,"
Trickster said.

Now the ducks followed Trickster and Fox into the lodge.
Loon shut the door behind them.
Loon stood watch.

Inside the lodge Trickster arranged the ducks in a circle.
"Let's do the shut-eye dance!" Trickster said.

"What's that?" one duck said. "What's the shut-eye dance?"

"You simply keep your eyes shut," Trickster said,
"and dance about.

I'll open my carry-sack,
our best, most powerful songs will fly out,
and you can dance to them."

"Ready?" said Fox.
"Ready!" all the ducks shouted.

"Shut your eyes," said Trickster.
All the ducks shut their eyes.

"This is a beautiful sight," Trickster said.
"Two things I especially love," said Fox.
"Marsh reeds swaying in the wind—
and a flock of ducks dancing with their eyes shut."

"Sing loudly now," said Trickster.
Fox sang loudly.

Just then the ducks heard, *Sqqqwwwkkkkchhhhkkkk!*
A choking sound, a strange, terrible choking sound
seemed to go right into their hearts!
"Is that choking sound part of your song?"
one shut-eye dancer cried out.
"Yes, it's part of our song," said Trickster.

"What language is Fox singing in?" another dancer asked.
"It's new to us."

Of course Trickster had just choked a duck,
but he said, "It's a language from a long time ago,
before you ducks were on the earth,
before I, your Big Brother, invented you ducks.
I know it sounds like choking,
but it's just an old-language song, that's all.
Don't worry. Keep doing the shut-eye dance."

Trickster buried the choked-to-death duck
feet-up in the ground.

Fox kept on singing loudly.
The shut-eye dancers stomped and spun about—
some got dizzy and bumped into each other,
but they were also laughing, having a good time,
and feeling proud that they could do a new dance so well.

Then: *Ssssqqccchhhkkkkwaaaakkk!*
Then: *Kkkkccchhhwwwwiiiwwkkchchch!*

Trickster buried two more shut-eye ducks,
their feet sticking up from the ground.
Outside, Loon pressed his ear to the lodge.
"It's getting quieter in there," he said.
"Fewer duck feet are dancing—I know it!"

Loon opened the door and caught Trickster choking a duck!
Loon flew at Trickster with his reed-cut beak
and hit Trickster straight-on in the forehead.
Trickster was knocked backward
and the choking duck escaped.
"Ducks, ducks, open your eyes!" cried Loon.
"Big Brother and Fox are making a meal of you!"

The rest of the shut-eye ducks opened their eyes.

"Run—fly off!" Loon shouted.
The ducks flew out the lodge door.

Just as Loon reached the door himself,
Trickster kicked him in the feet—
which is why, it is said, since that day
all loons have such flat feet.
Fox kicked Loon in the rear end—*Whap!*—
which is why, it is said, since that day
all loons have such ruffled tail feathers.

Ruffled, sore-footed Loon flew fast to the far end of the marsh,
where he joined the ducks.
All night they wept and wept and wept
for their companions choked by Trickster.
"It's my fault," said Loon.
"I shouldn't have let you dance."

"No, no, it's our fault," a duck said,
"for trusting Big Brother and Fox."

"It was fun dancing, until the choking started,"
one fledgling duck said.

"I'll admit that's true," another duck said.
"But the lesson is, we must do only our own dances,
hidden deep in the reeds, or safely out on the marsh,
and with our eyes open!"

"I prefer to dance out in the middle of a lake," Loon said.
"At night. Or sometimes at dawn or dusk."

Back in the lodge,
duck feathers were still swirling to the ground.
"Well," said Fox, "at least we have three ducks to eat."
Three pairs of duck feet were sticking up from the ground.
"Let's roast them up and eat them
and rub duck grease in our hair
so as to remember the taste of ducks
long after we've eaten them."

"Wait," said Trickster. "We can't just eat ducks like this."

"Hey, hey," said Fox.
"If you've been doing the shut-eye dance with ducks,
it makes you hungry for ducks.
Let's pull these three ducks up by their feet and feast!"

"Don't be in such a hurry," said Trickster.
"First we need some other-side-of-the-marsh sweet grass
to sprinkle on these ducks while we roast them.
Fox, you go gather some other-side-of-the-marsh sweet grass."

"Where do I find it?" said Fox.

Trickster said, "It's called other-side-of-the-marsh sweet grass."

"Oh, now I get it," Fox said.

"OK, run and get some sweet grass,
and when you bring it back, I'll chop it up properly
and sprinkle it on the ducks.
I'll have them all prepared to cook by the time you return."

Fox set out, moving through the edge reeds
to find the other-side-of-the-marsh sweet grass.

Quickly now, quickly now, Trickster built a fire,
pulled up all three ducks by their feet,
roasted them,
and made a hearty meal.
He doused the fire.
He threw the charred logs into the woods
and swept away all the ashes.
Then he stuck the duck feet back in the ground
so it appeared as though the whole ducks were still buried.
Trickster lay against the wall of the lodge.
He snored and snored, pretending to sleep.

When Fox got to the other side of the marsh,
he started tasting a blade of each kind of grass.

"No, this one's not sweet," he said.
"This one's quite bitter.
This one tastes awful.
Nothing sweet yet.
This one's good for making a whistling sound through,
but it's not sweet."
Fox tasted stalks, reeds, grasses.
None of it was sweet.
None of it was other-side-of-the-marsh sweet grass.

Just then Loon landed with a splash nearby.
"Fox—fool!" Loon said. "Fox—fool! Fox—fool!
You worked so hard to capture ducks to eat,
but you're still hungry, aren't you?
But guess what? Our Big Brother is stuffed!"

Fox leaped at the loon—but Loon easily flew off,
cackling and echoing his laughter.
Fox scrambled back onto dry land and ran back to the lodge.

When Fox burst through the door, he saw the duck feet.
"Friend, Big Brother, wake up!" he said.
Trickster pretended to wake up.
"Where's the sweet grass?" Trickster said.

"I couldn't find any," Fox said.
"Let's eat these ducks without sweet grass.
I don't mind. I'm hungry."

"I've been thinking," said Trickster.
"You were such a great help in capturing these ducks,
I'm going to leave them all for you."

"Why, thank you, Big Brother," said Fox.

"But don't start to eat the ducks
until I am well out of sight," said Trickster.
"Because it's true, I too am hungry
and the sight of you feasting on ducks—
the smell of ducks roasting on a fire—
might make me change my mind!"

"All right, I'll wait," said Fox.
"Good luck in your travels, then, Big Brother."

Trickster set out walking.
Still close enough for the fox to see him,
Trickster turned to look back.
Through the open door of the reed lodge, he saw Fox.

There sat Fox, next to three pairs of duck feet
sticking up from the ground.
"Poor Fox," Trickster said quietly.
"If you sit with duck feet long enough,
you get very hungry for ducks."

Trickster hurried on—
he didn't want to be anywhere close by
when Fox discovered that the ducks were gone.

After that, news of Trickster's betrayal
traveled far and wide among foxes.
Foxes never were Trickster's travel companions again,
so it is said.

Trickster Tells Whiskey Jack the Truth

Whiskey Jack was a complainer—a *complaint* bird!
Flitting from tree to tree, hopping along the ground,
Whiskey Jack squawked his loud complaints.
In winter Whiskey Jack said, "It's too cold!"
In summer Whiskey Jack said, "It's too hot!"

One day, just between winter and summer,
Trickster made camp near some thawing marshes.
The ice was fast breaking up.
Soon the summer birds would arrive.

As soon as Trickster built a fire,
Whiskey Jack landed nearby on the ground.
"Here're my troubles," Whiskey Jack said.
"I don't like my tail—it's too short.
I don't like my wings—they're too small.
Nobody ever says, 'Hey, Whiskey Jack, you're beautiful.
Hey, hey, Whiskey Jack, come over here and marry me!'
My head's too big for my body!"

"Whiskey Jack, shut up!" Trickster cried out.
"I can hear that you aren't satisfied.
And do you know what I think of that?
I think, *Too bad!*
Good-bye!"

Trickster doused the fire and set out walking.
He was going to circle the marshes,
watching the ice break up
and scanning the sky for summer birds.

"You're just going to walk away?" Whiskey Jack said.
"But I'm not done complaining yet!
Listen, I don't like the way I fly.
I don't like my voice.
I don't like my feathers."

Trickster stopped in his tracks, turned around,
and said, "Whiskey Jack, why not borrow some feathers?
Soon a lot of summer birds will be here.
Soon the big meeting of the birds will take place.
Go to the meeting. Ask for feathers."

Whiskey Jack flew into the woods to think this over.

Days went by.
More days.
Still more days went by.
Trickster walked and walked and walked.
He walked entirely around the marshes.
When he got back to his old camp,
it was summer.
The sky was filled with birds flying in to the marshes.

Whiskey Jack landed at Trickster's feet.
"Time for the big meeting of birds,"
Trickster said. "How about it,
are you going to ask to borrow feathers?"

In the past Whiskey Jack had kept shy of the other birds.
He was too vain—he hid out.
Now he voiced his worries to Trickster.
"The others might mock my beak.
They might mock my wings,
my tail feathers,
my way of flying.
They might mock my voice!"

"*Please* just go borrow new feathers!" said Trickster.
Trickster picked up Whiskey Jack and flung him into the air.

Whiskey Jack flew right in
and landed amidst the summer birds.

Whiskey Jack walked up to a teal.
"Can I borrow some tail feathers?" said Whiskey Jack.
"Sure, sure, sure," the teal said.
The teal reached back, plucked out a few tail feathers,
and handed them to Whiskey Jack.
Whiskey Jack stuck the teal's feathers into his own backside.

Then bold Whiskey Jack walked up to a grebe.
"Can I borrow some wing feathers?" asked Whiskey Jack.
"Fine by me," the grebe said.
The grebe stretched out a wing
and Whiskey Jack yanked out a few feathers.
Then he stuck the grebe's feathers into his own wings.

"Hey, hey, can I borrow some neck feathers from you?"
Whiskey Jack said to a goose. "You've got a lot.
I just need five or six for my own neck."
"I can spare some," the goose said.
The goose slid out a bunch of neck feathers
and gave them to Whiskey Jack.
Whiskey Jack stuck the goose feathers into his own neck.
Whiskey Jack was borrowing feathers like crazy.

Now all the birds gathered for the meeting.
They certainly were surprised when Whiskey Jack sauntered in.
"Fancy seeing you here!" a crane said.
"You've always shunned us in the past," a heron said.
Whiskey Jack strutted about,
preening, bragging up his new feathers.
"I'm sleek," he said.
"I'm beautiful.
Look at me! Look at me! Look at me!"
Whiskey Jack thought he cut a fine figure.

OK, so now the meeting was about to begin.
Trickster kept to his camp.
This meeting was for birds only.
Many secrets would be exchanged
and nobody but birds could hear them.
It has always been that way.
Human beings can watch from a distance.
Moose, wolves, bears, lynx, hare,
frogs, turtles, fishers, mice, wolverines, and mink—
all can watch from a distance.
But only summer birds take part in the meeting.

Whiskey Jack shouted, "Let's get this meeting started!
I'm here now, let's get started.
Let me hear some grebe secrets.
Let me hear some crane secrets.
Let's talk over some loon secrets.
Go on, go on, let the secrets fly!
How about some heron and diver-duck secrets?"

But when the meeting started up,
Whiskey Jack didn't quite know what to do.

Some birds startled up right in front of him
and flew off to the north, then turned sharply back.
Other birds circled the marshes high in the air,
dived, then skidded across the water.
Everywhere at once, Whiskey Jack heard
squawking, keening, honking, splashing.

Birds flew south and back,
west and east and back.
There was much commotion.

Secrets were flying every which way,
but Whiskey Jack didn't catch a single one,
and nobody talked to him.
Whiskey Jack was befuddled.

And suddenly the meeting was over.
The summer birds drifted off to the farthest marsh.
Whiskey Jack stood there by himself.

Trickster stepped out of some tall reeds.
"Let's have a meeting just between you and me,"
he said to Whiskey Jack.
"Now that you've got new tail, neck, and wing feathers,
let's see you fly!"

Whiskey Jack got up his nerve,
took off, and started to fly.
But right away his flying got clumsy.
He somersaulted directly into a tree branch.
He fell. He walked dizzily.

"Well, I'm a miserable sight, aren't I?" he said.
"Try and get those borrowed feathers off," Trickster said.
"Truth is, you flew much better without them.
Truth is, they look ridiculous on you.
Truth is, the other birds don't like you much at all."

Whiskey Jack plucked out the feathers one by one,
crying, "Ouch! Ouch! Ouch!"
until all the borrowed feathers scattered in the wind.
Then Whiskey Jack flew into the woods.
But he still kept whacking into trees!
"I'm hitting trees!" he complained.
"I'm hurt! I'm falling dizzily!
I'm wobbly getting up!
There, I've flown into yet another tree!
This is the worst day of my life!"

"Stop flying for a while!" Trickster yelled out.
"You'll kill yourself! I'll think how to help you.
Just sit tight."

Whiskey Jack sat brooding in the woods for a few days.
Then Trickster found him and said,
"Whiskey Jack, you're a foolish bird.
I know that you're lonely.
That's one thing a terribly lonely bird does,
crashes into trees.
So here's what:
I'll tell the people who live around here
to welcome you into their camps.
They'll let you come around for scraps of food.
They'll invite you in for gossip.
But be prepared: They'll throw dirt or snow at you
if you complain one time too many!"

Whiskey Jack flew out into the open.
"Ah, I see you're flying pretty well again already,"
Trickster said. "Are you still dizzy? How are you feeling?"

"Those summer birds were rude!" Whiskey Jack said.
"I've got secrets I'll never tell them,
no matter how much they beg!
A few of those birds smelled pretty bad, too.
It looks like a storm's coming in.
Why do I have to get wet when it rains?
I don't like getting wet!"

Trickster couldn't stand it anymore.
He grabbed Whiskey Jack and took him to the nearest village.
"Good luck!" he said to Whiskey Jack.
"Good luck!" he said to the villagers.

Trickster ran back to the marshes
to see the summer birds fill the air at dusk.

That is what happened:
Trickster helped Whiskey Jack.
To this very day, Whiskey Jack is a clumsy flier.
He's got ruffled feathers.
He doesn't go near other birds.
But you can always find him around human villages,
especially at mealtimes.
Whiskey Jack will flit in for scraps,
snap up a crust here, a piece of fat there,
and fly off.
From a tree or from atop a tent, he'll complain,
"Hey, is that all I get?
How about some more?
I'm here. I'm here. I'm here.
Hey, listen up,
I'm talking!"

Trickster and the Walking Contest

Trickster wanted to travel with a wolverine.
Wolverines had the reputation as the best walkers
in the territory.
They could walk all day—
the sun got worn out watching a wolverine walk.
They could walk all night—
the moon got worn out watching a wolverine walk.
"I can outwalk a wolverine!"
Trickster bragged to himself at the beginning of winter.
"Wolverine!" he shouted toward the forest.
"Let's have a walking contest!"

But no wolverine answered.
"I know you're out there, Wolverine!" Trickster called.

Trickster went walking.
It was snowing.
It became deep winter.
"I'm lonely—I'm tired of traveling alone," Trickster shouted.

Right away a tribe of ice owls landed near Trickster.
These owls looked like snowy owls,
but they were made of ice and showed up only in winter.
You could put an ice owl into a soup cauldron over a fire,
and it would melt into owl water.
Ice owls stayed well away from soup cauldrons,
campfires, human lodges with wood-burning stoves.
The colder it got, the happier ice owls became.

"Big Brother," an ice owl said, "why not travel with us?
This is going to be the most terrible winter in memory.
We'll teach you a lot about how to survive."

"Who's the best at getting through bad winters?"
Trickster asked.

"Wolverines," the ice owls said.

"I want to travel with a wolverine, then," Trickster said.

"Try and find one!" an ice owl said.

Well, Trickster and the ice owls traveled together.
And the ice owls were right: It was a terrible winter.
There were ice storms every other day,
and icicles hung from the moon.

The ice owls were good to Trickster.
They taught him many useful things.

Now, in the past,
ice owls had had terrible run-ins with wolverines.
They had been ambushed and eaten by wolverines.
One time a wolverine had sauntered off
with an ice owl wing in its jaws
and could be heard gnawing on it for a long time.
Ice owls hated even to hear the word *wolverine*.

But Trickster kept saying, "I want to travel with a wolverine.
I want to outwalk a wolverine,"
which annoyed the ice owls.

"Stop saying that name!" the ice owls shouted.

One evening just after dusk,
they came upon a hunting camp.
There was one lodge.
They got up close to the lodge.
They listened and heard human voices.
"Let's go inside and ransack this lodge," said Trickster.
"I smell moose meat cooking over the fire.
I'm hungry. Let's go inside."

"But there's a *fire* in there!" an ice owl said.

"Stay back from the fire; I'll douse it," said Trickster.
"Then it'll be dark.
You swoop in, and grab the moose meat,
and fly out to the trees."

"All right," said an ice owl.

Trickster flung open the entrance-hide to the lodge
and ran inside.
The ice owls followed close behind.

Suddenly Trickster turned,
grabbed an ice owl,
and flung the owl into the fire—*Hsssssssssssss!*
The ice owl melted and doused the fire,
and it was dark inside the lodge.
People were running every which way.
Trickster shouted, "Grab the moose meat!"
In the dark, he heard the beating of ice owl wings.
Then the hide-flap opened,
and Trickster saw the ice owls flee with the moose meat
held between their beaks.

Trickster ran after the owls but couldn't catch them.

In the woods, Trickster built a cooking fire.
He sat close, waiting for the ice owls.
Finally an ice owl appeared at the edge of the woods.

"You betrayed us, Big Brother!" the owl said.
"We are going to cold caves far away—
only a wolverine knows where to find such caves."

The ice owl flew off.
In the distance Trickster saw the other ice owls fly off.

He sat by the cooking fire
with no food to eat.

Next morning Trickster went walking over a snowy field.
Soon he heard something under the snow.
It was a sound he had never heard before.

The sound was tunneling along, *Snap, snap, snap. . . .*
The sound went off to the south
and Trickster followed it.
Snap, snap, snap, it went along under the snow.

"Wolverine, is that you?" Trickster spoke to the snow.
The snow did not answer.
Trickster went walking.

He grew cold. He started to shiver.
He needed to find a warm place.
He was hungry.
Just then he saw a young deer.
"I'll eat this deer," he said.
"Then I'll make a coat of its hide and keep warm."
Just as Trickster was about to leap on the deer,
there was an explosion of snow!
Snow flew up in a blinding cloud,
and when the cloud settled
the deer was gone!

Trickster walked to where the deer had stood.
At his feet he saw the opening to a tunnel in the snow.
"I'm not going down there," Trickster said.
He went walking.

As he walked,
Trickster heard another sound under the snow.
He leaned down to listen.
He heard, *Crunch, crunch, crunch. . . .*

"Wolverine, is that you crunching on deer bones?"
Trickster said into the snow.

The snow did not answer.

"That's the second time I've talked to snow," Trickster said.
"And the second time the rude snow did not answer!"
Trickster went walking.

Trickster walked all day and into the night.
Finally, he saw another lodge.
He listened at its walls.
He heard people talking inside.
They were talking about geese—*summer* birds.
They were talking about ducks—*summer* birds.
They were talking about gnats—*summer* insects.
They were slapping—*Slap, slap, slap.*
They said, "Get away, mosquitoes!"
The people were talking about summer things,
while all around Trickster it was snowing heavily.
Icicles hung from the full moon.
Trickster was shivering outside the lodge.

Suddenly a wolverine rushed past Trickster and into the lodge!
Trickster watched as the wolverine
gnarled up every last pair of snowshoes,
then gnarled up all the blankets,
then gnarled up the hunting rifles,
then doused the woodstove fire with snarling spit,
then warned the people,
"Don't talk about summer things in the middle of winter!
Winter is the season when I get to tunnel in snow.
Winter is when I do my best walking.
I like winter!
Don't talk about summer things in the middle of winter.
It puts me in a bad mood."

"All right, we've learned our lesson," the people said.
"Here, take some caribou, beaver, and moose meat!"

"Very well," the wolverine said.
The wolverine took the gift-offering and ran from the lodge.

"Wait!" cried Trickster. "I'll travel with you!"

"I like to travel alone," said Wolverine.

But Trickster did not want to miss his chance
to outwalk a wolverine
and ran to catch up.

The wolverine stayed well ahead.
Trickster heard the wolverine snarling out words,
"Snowdrifts,
snow blindness,
snow squalls,
snow, snow, snow . . ."

Trickster followed the wolverine for many days.
This was the walking contest Trickster had always wanted.

Trickster finally said, "Let's both rest."
"I'm nowhere near tired yet," said the wolverine.

They walked for two days and nights.

"Let's take a rest," Trickster said.
"Walk a little faster," said the wolverine,
"come on, come on, come on!"

At dawn Trickster said, "Let's rest."
But the wolverine was too far ahead to hear him.

Trickster sat down in the snow.

The wolverine walked over a snowy hill of trees.
The wolverine was traveling north into north
into north
into north
into north.

Trickster and the Clacking Sleeves

There's good luck in fishing,
there's bad luck in fishing,
and the village called Otter Lake was having good luck.
Fish were drying on smoke racks.
Fish were in the soup.
Fish were being cooked over a fire.
The good smell of smoke-drying fish drifted out into the trees,
where Trickster smelled it and got hungry.

I'll just make a visit to this village,
get myself something to eat, Trickster thought.
He walked into the village.
"How about some fish for me to eat?" he said.
And right away the oldest woman in the village
brought Trickster the biggest trout.
Trickster ate it.
"You can stay here with us until nighttime,"
the woman said. "Then—leave."

When it grew dark, Trickster set out from the village,
but he hid in the trees
and waited for everyone to fall asleep.
When the village was asleep, he crept back
and ate all the fish.

He tore them from the smoke-drying racks.
He lifted the pot of soup to his mouth, tipped it back,
and gulped it to the bottom.
He ate every last fish.

He was just about to flee the village
when the oldest woman stepped from her lodge and said,
"In which direction are you going to travel, Big Brother?"

"East," said Trickster.

"Well, good luck then," the old woman said.

She sat in the middle of the village,
gathering up fish heads, fish tails, fish skeletons.
She started to sew them together into a coat.
"Yes, good luck.
But my messenger crow brought news of hazards
in the easterly direction.

"My crow said there were many suckholes,
quicksand, ankle-grabbing mud,
all in the easterly direction.
A lot of people were sucked under.
A lot of people had their ankles roughly grabbed by mud.
A lot of people disappeared into quicksand.
Terrible rains must have fallen out there."

"You're angry because I ate all of the fish," Trickster said. "So you're trying to scare me."

"Well," the old woman said, "my crow has never lied." She went back to work on her fish coat.

Trickster set out to the east.
There was a clear, blue sky—
then it was a dark, roiling sky.
Suddenly Trickster said, "I feel shorter."

He was up to his neck in suckhole mud!

The messenger crow flew over.
"*Awwgggghhhh!* Big Brother," the crow called down, "do you need help?"

"I'm ashamed to be helped by a lowly crow," Trickster said. "But I suppose it'll be something for you to brag about."

The crow lifted Trickster from the mud.
Dripping mud, Trickster went back to Otter Lake.

"I've had a bad time," Trickster said to the old woman.
"I had to be rescued by a crow.
I'm tired. I'm hungry.
Give me some fish!"

The old woman tossed him a fish tail and a few fish bones.
"This is all you've left us," she said.
Trickster picked at the bones.

The old woman had finished a fish-head-and-bone sleeve.
Trickster set out.

"Big Brother," the old woman said,
"in which direction are you going?"

"To the west," Trickster said.

"To the west!" the old woman said.
"My crow said that ashes were getting caught
in everyone's throat—
people, animals—in the westerly direction.
Big fires out there. Ashes caught in everyone's throat.
Well, good luck in your travels, Big Brother."

"One scare was true—two scares can't be!" said Trickster.
He set out to the west.

He walked under clear skies. No wind, not even a breeze.
And then Trickster began to cross a stream
and saw ashes on the water.

He got to the dry ground.
Ashes swirled in the air;
small fires were burning—
it looked as if a forest fire
had recently passed through.
He heard a fox coughing.
He heard a beaver coughing.
He heard a fisher coughing.
He heard—*himself* coughing!
He was choking on ashes.
Ashes worked down into his throat, ears, nose,
until he cried out, "I'm choking on ashes!
I can't hear; I can't smell because of ashes!"

The crow flew down and hovered right next to Trickster
and shouted, "Big Brother, let me help you!"

The crow got the ashes out of Trickster's ears.
"This is an interesting place," the crow said.
"Ashes, coughing, smoke,
eerie quiet after a forest fire has raged through.
But you don't seem to get on well here, Big Brother.
You're choking on ashes.
The fox coughs but doesn't choke.
The beaver coughs but doesn't choke.
The fisher coughs but doesn't choke.
But you're choking to death.
I'd better help you out."

The crow lugged in a carry-sack of water
and doused Trickster,
washed him free of ashes.
He filled the carry-sack again
and let Trickster drink, drink, drink.
Trickster drank five carry-sacks of water.

"I guess you'll brag about saving my life," Trickster said.
"People will start calling me 'Saved-Twice-By-A-Lowly-Crow.'"

Trickster went back to Otter Lake.
The old woman had finished the back of the coat.
"Welcome back, Big Brother," she said. "You must be hungry."
Trickster took a bite from the sleeve.
"That's how hungry I am!" he said.

"Luck would have it, some ashes drifted in
from the westerly direction," the old woman said.
"I can fix you up some ash broth.
Maybe I'll add some fish scales.
That's about all we have to eat around here
until the villagers are able to catch more fish."

Trickster set out.
"I see you're going north," the old woman said.

"That's right," said Trickster.

"Good luck, good luck, good luck," she said.
"Because my crow told me that the close-eye sleet
is not too far north of here.
My crow said that if a traveler comes along,
sleet throws itself at the traveler.
It closes up a traveler's eyes.
It beats and stings against a traveler's face and hands.
You can't fight it.
Close-eye sleet is the worst."

"Your first scare was true," said Trickster.
"Your second scare was true.
But now you're lying! Your messenger crow is lying!"

He set out to the north.

Beautiful, clear sky.
Good luck in walking—then suddenly bad luck.
The sound of a hush, *Shhhhhh*—
"Sleet is far away," Trickster said,
and then he was ambushed by sleet!

It happened fast.
This was the close-eye sleet!
Freezing cold sleet stung Trickster's face and hands.
"No—stop!" Trickster shouted,
but his voice was swallowed up by the howling sleet.
"This sleet is my death!" Trickster cried.

Just then the crow landed on Trickster's shoulder.
If any voice can get through howling sleet, it's a crow's.
Crow stuck his beak right into Trickster's ear.
"Hey—*Awwwwgggggghhhh!*—Big Brother, let me help you!
This is the very worst close-eye sleet I've ever seen.
Let me help you!"

The crow lifted Trickster away from the sleet
and carried him back to the village.
The crow dropped Trickster next to the old woman.
She had just finished the other sleeve of the fish coat.

"Welcome back, Big Brother," she said. "Sit here by the fire.
Rub your hands together. Thaw out.
Make yourself comfortable.
In a little while, you'll be able to open your eyes again."

Trickster sat there with his eyes swollen closed.
He heard the old woman stitching.
He heard the fish bones clack together.
Trickster was sleet-blind for the rest of the night.

At dawn the villagers woke up.
The old woman said, "Trickster ate all of our fish!"
People right away went out fishing.
Some had good luck, some had bad luck.

Trickster still couldn't open his eyes.
But he smelled fish being smoked on the smoke racks.
He smelled fish soup.
He smelled roasting fish.

Finally the old woman fit the fish-head-and-bones coat
over Trickster.
"Here, Big Brother," she said. "Please accept our gift.
Wear it always. It will help you remember our village!"

Trickster stood up.
Now he was able to open his eyes.

Suddenly the moldy fish heads started to clack their jaws!
Every step that Trickster took his sleeves clacked wildly—
Clack, clack, clack, clack!
He tried to spin out of the coat, but he couldn't get it off.
Clack, clack, clack, clack, clack, clack, clack!

"When you get to the first big river in the southerly direction," the old woman said, "you'll be able to take off this coat."

She handed Trickster a carry-sack full of new-caught fish.

"Good luck in your travels!" the old woman said.
Then the villagers kicked Trickster out.

Trickster went walking.
There were clear skies—some dried mud slid from his ankles.
There were more clear skies—
he picked some ashes from his hair.
There were more clear skies—he rubbed his sore eyes.
And *Clack, clack, clack, clack, clack!*
His sleeves just wouldn't shut up, all the way to the river.

Trickster got out of the coat and crossed the river.
When he turned to look back,
there was the messenger crow—many crows, in fact—
sitting on the coat.

The wind carried the crow's conversation to Trickster.
"Look, across the river, it's who we call Big Brother!"
one crow said.

"I call him 'Saved-Three-Times-By-A-Crow,'"
said the messenger crow.

Trickster and the Night-Tailed Weasels

One night Trickster was walking across a frozen lake.
Up ahead he saw a black tail-tip moving across the lake.
Trickster knew right away
the tail-tip was attached to the tail of a short-tail weasel.
Short-tail weasels turn all white in winter,
except for their tail-tips.

"Tail-tip, which night are you?" Trickster called out,
for he knew that each weasel's black tail-tip
was a way for weasels to remember a night
on which something important happened.
"Weasel," Trickster shouted,
"which night do you have waving on your tail-tip?"
His voice echoed.

The short-tail weasel whose tail was waving stopped.
"Big Brother," the weasel said, "you take a guess.
But if you guess wrong—or lie—
I'll thin the ice around you, and if you try to walk farther,
you'll fall through."

The weasel waved its tail a little more.

Trickster quickly said, "It's the night three winters ago
when I made many hare come around
so that you weasels could have a feast!
There was a terrible blizzard
and you weasels were starving.
I couldn't just let you go hungry!
You all cried, 'Big Brother, our ribs are showing!
Help us out!'
So I worked some magic
and made a lot of hare appear,
sliding about on the lake ice,
leaping from their snow huts.
You weasels chased them down.
There was plenty to eat."

Hearing this, the short-tail weasel chattered,
"*Chhhh Cchhh Chhhh*—That's a lie!"
and thinned the ice around Trickster.
It made a loud cracking sound.

"Listen up!" the weasel said.
"Waving on my tail-tip is the night you came by,
Big Brother, and grabbed all the hare for yourself!
It's true, there was a blizzard.
It's true, we weasels were starving.
But you walked right past us
with the hare slung across your back!"

There was bright moonlight
and snow-glare light;
Trickster could see many tail-tips waving above the lake.

Many weasels had arrived.

Now another weasel spoke. "Listen up, Big Brother!
At the end of my tail I'm waving a night
on which you became a snow snake.
You hissed and swirled us weasels across the lake for fun.
You chased us half the night.
When you left, we lay panting on the ice,
breath-clouds freezing on our faces,
too tired even to crawl away.
Owls swooped down
and plucked up a few of us in their beaks
and flew off into the trees.
We won't forget that night.
We still weep over that night."

"No. That wasn't me," Trickster cried out. "Not me!"
More ice thinned and cracked near Trickster.

Then, one by one,
the weasels said to Trickster, "Listen up!"
and each told the story of its tail-tip.

Standing on thin ice,
shaking his head back and forth,
Trickster kept saying, "No, no, no, it wasn't like that.
I never did those things."

But the weasels were telling Trickster the truth all right.

Finally Trickster shouted,
"Give me those nights back!
I want those nights back!"

With that, a weasel said,
"No, Big Brother,
those nights are ours now.
Those nights belong to us weasels now."

The ice was cracking all around.
Trickster didn't know what to do.
He grew frightened.
Soon he would be flailing about in freezing water!

Trickster turned himself into a winter weasel.
He was a short-tail weasel now.
He had a black tail-tip.
He began scampering over the cracking ice,
light, light on his small feet, toward the snowbank.
When he reached the hard-packed snow,
he turned back into Trickster again.
But his weasel tail, with its black tip, stayed on him!

Now the weasels appeared all throughout the trees!

One weasel told Trickster,
"You have this very night already on your tail-tip!"

All the weasels rolled in the snow,
laughed, chattered their teeth,
waved their tail-tips.
Trickster ran off
and did not stop running for many days and nights.

One day he happened upon some wolves.
"Big Brother," a wolf said, "how did you get that tail?"

Trickster said, "Well, my friends the weasels,
whom I kept from starving,
gave me this black tail-tip
because they love me so much
and are so grateful to me!"

But then a weasel popped right up from a snow tunnel
and said, "Listen up, wolves!
I'll tell you what happened
on the night waving on Trickster's tail!"
And the weasel told the truth.

Trickster set out walking.
He was walking by moonlight
when a snowy owl whisked past,
barely touching Trickster with its wings.
"Owl, come back, admire my tail!" Trickster called out.
The owl turned midflight
and landed near Trickster.
"A very nice weasel tail," the owl said. "How'd you get it?"

Trickster looked around
to see if a weasel was anywhere to be seen.
He saw the owl.
He saw snow.
He saw the moon.
He saw the trees.
No weasel.
"During a terrible blizzard
I helped weasels get hare to eat,"
Trickster bragged.

"They were so grateful, they gave me this tail.
Now we're dear friends."
From inside a clump of snow low on a spruce tree
a weasel suddenly flung itself to the ground.
"Owl, listen up!" the weasel said.
"And keep away from me with that sharp beak.
I'm going to tell you how our Big Brother really got his tail!"

And so it went.
Day after day,
night after night,
Trickster couldn't shake loose from the weasels.

Then one night Trickster had a dream.
In the dream, every weasel chattered,
"You were cruel to us! It was you! It was you! It was you!"
They bit his feet.
They bit his ears.
They bit his knees.

Trickster startled awake, shouting,
"All right, I'll leave you weasels alone!"
It had been the worst dream of weasels he'd ever had.

Then he noticed that his black tail-tip was gone.

During the next winter,
Trickster did not hoard food from weasels
or turn into a snow snake
and hiss weasels over the frozen lake.

But the winter after that,
he did.

Trickster and the Fainting Birds

Trickster was sleeping poorly.
Well, to tell the truth, he wasn't sleeping at all.
It wasn't the buzzing of mosquitoes that kept him awake.
It wasn't the windy rain that kept him awake.
He just couldn't sleep.
"It's not fleas or blackflies or rocks sticking into my back
when I lie on the ground," he said. "I just can't sleep!"

Trickster set out walking.
He walked and walked.
Finally he came to a people's village.
This was near a place call Burntwood River.
There were lightning-singed trees all along the riverbanks.
It was nighttime; there was a big moon.
Trickster stood at the edge of the village.

There was something exciting going on amongst the villagers.
Trickster drew closer.

Then he crawled inside a lightning-singed tree stump.
From inside the tree stump,
he saw that a sleepwalking contest was going on.

To start with, a beautiful young woman
was led out to the middle of the village by her father.
She was asleep.
"Whichever man sleepwalks better than my daughter,"
the father said, "will get to marry her. She's agreed to this."

The girl's father took out a flute and played it.
The girl began to sleepwalk.
She sleepwalked a few steps,
then she tossed herself about the village—
wild leaps, somersaults, rolling—
then she walked on her hands.
"Even I've never seen her walk on her hands before!"
the father said.
Everyone was greatly impressed.

"All right," said the father,
"who'd like to try to marry my daughter?"

A young man began to sleepwalk.
At first he was helped along by his sister,
but then she let him go on his own.
But right away this man stumbled into a tree.
He woke up, crying, "That's the same tree I always run into!"
There was much laughter.
He stood by the tree.
He didn't get to marry the young woman.

Then a very old, wrinkled man sleepwalked.

He had had a lot of practice,
and he sleepwalked well
until he fell over a camp dog—
the dog yelped and snarled the old man awake.
He woke up with the dog's face close to his.
There was much laughter.
The old man said, "Well, I've already had two wives.
I shouldn't be too selfish!"
There was more laughter.
He didn't get to marry the young woman.

Over to one side of the village,
the young woman's father was holding her tightly
to keep her from tossing about, somersaulting, and rolling.
He was getting tired. The young woman was very strong.
"Hurry up—someone sleepwalk!
I'm afraid my daughter will fling herself into the river!
I'm about to wake her up!"

Watching all of this, Trickster thought, *I'd like a wife—
yes, I'll marry this beautiful young woman!*
But just when he was about to shout, "It's my turn!"
and jump asleep out of the burnt tree stump,
a handsome young man sleepwalked out
to the middle of the village.
Nobody was helping the young man—
and he was excellent at sleepwalking.

First he added some sticks to the fire,
walked over to the young woman, took her by the hand,
and led her to the cooking fire.
They both warmed themselves there.
Then he cooked some fish soup.

Next he strung bear claws into a necklace
and put the necklace around the young woman's neck.
He chopped wood and put logs on the fire.
He mended a pair of snowshoes.
He did all these things while asleep.
The contest was over.
"Surely this young man will marry my daughter!"
the father said.

The father woke his daughter, then woke the young man.
"Who is to marry me?" the daughter asked.

Trickster leaped from the tree stump.
"I am!" he shouted.

"No—this young man will marry my daughter!" the father said.
Trickster turned the father into a kingfisher.
Just like that!
The kingfisher-father flew up to a branch over the river.

"It doesn't matter if my father-in-law is a kingfisher,"
the handsome young man said. "I'll still marry his daughter!"
Trickster turned the young man into a kingfisher.
The kingfisher-young-man flew up
and sat alongside the kingfisher-father.

"Turn them back!" the young woman cried.
"If you marry me," said Trickster,
"I'll turn them back into people."
"No!" the young woman said.

Hearing this, Trickster caused the kingfisher-father to faint.
The kingfisher-father tumbled through the air
and into the river.
Right away the kingfisher-young-man dived into the river
and carried the kingfisher-father back up to the branch.

"I will make those two kingfishers faint off the branch
all day, all night, all day again,
unless you marry me," said Trickster.

"I won't marry you," the young woman said.
Trickster made the kingfisher-young-man
faint off the branch into the river.

The kingfisher-father—who had gathered back his strength—
dived in and carried the kingfisher-young-man
up to the branch.

"Now marry me," Trickster said.

"No!" said the young woman.

Then Trickster made the two kingfishers
faint into the river at the same time.
The young woman dived right in
and—holding a kingfisher in each hand—swam back to shore.
The kingfishers flew from her hands up to their branch.

"It twists your heart
watching kingfishers faint off a branch,
doesn't it?" Trickster said to the young woman.
"Marry me, and you won't ever again see kingfishers faint."

"I'd rather marry a kingfisher
and have a kingfisher-father,
even if both faint away and drown in the river,
than marry you!" the young woman said.
"In fact, I have always preferred kingfishers to people.
I have preferred kingfishers to people since I was a little girl.
So you have made me very happy—
I'm going to marry that kingfisher right now
and have a kingfisher-father!"

There was a quick wedding—
the young woman married the kingfisher-young-man.
"I've never been happier!" she said.
"I'll have kingfisher-children
and raise them by the river."

Seeing how happy the young woman was
made Trickster even more jealous.

He turned himself into a kingfisher
and flew up to the branch!

Then he made the two other kingfishers dive into the river.
This time they did not faint—
they dived like any kingfisher would.
But when they flew up to the branch,
each had a fish impaled by its beak—
their beaks had stuck through the fish.

Quickly, each fish dried hard as stone.
The kingfisher-father and the kingfisher-young-man
could not pry the fish off.
Trickster-kingfisher now dived into the river.
He came up with a fish and ate it on the branch.
"These other kingfishers can't open their beaks,"
Trickster-kingfisher said to the young woman.
"They can't catch fish. They'll starve.
To watch a kingfisher not catch fish twists your heart.
What's more, since you prefer kingfishers to people,
what if I turn them back into people?
Then I'll be the only kingfisher in the village—
you can marry me!"

"No!" said the young woman.

A day went by, then another;
then two more days went by.
Each night the young woman slept by the river.
Kingfisher-father and kingfisher-young-man
were getting weaker.
Little moans and cries came from their throats.
Trickster-kingfisher was catching a lot of fish
and feasting on them.

"One more day," Trickster-kingfisher said to the young woman,
"and these other kingfishers will faint from hunger.
You could stop that.
All you have to do is marry me."

"As soon as they faint into the river and drown,"
the young woman said, "I will climb that tree,
sit on the branch, and stop eating.
Soon I'll faint into the river and drown."

Hearing this, Trickster-kingfisher knew he couldn't win.
He turned himself back into Trickster.
"There're too many kingfishers here for my liking!"
he said. "And I don't want to get married anyway!"

He went walking.
He walked all day.
He lay down on the ground but couldn't sleep.
He walked all night.
He lay down again.
"I still can't sleep," he said.
"Can't sleep, can't sleep, can't sleep."

Trickster never did turn the kingfishers back into people.
The young woman was able to pry the fish from their beaks.
She fed them bits of fish and they grew strong.
Soon they were able to fend for themselves.
The young woman stayed married to the kingfisher.
And she had kingfisher-children,
who never once fainted from the branch.
In winter her children flew far away.
In summer they came back.
Every summer for the rest of her life,
the woman slept by the river.
She had many kingfisher-grandchildren, too.

This happened a long time ago.
But the lightning-singed stumps by the Burntwood River
still smell burnt to this day.

Story Notes

Trickster and the Best Hermit

I worked on "Trickster and the Best Hermit" with Abraham Little, a French Canadian/Cree, in Flin Flon, Manitoba. I had only five or six days with Abraham Little; during that period we got four versions of "Trickster and the Best Hermit" down on paper, and my rendition includes all the episodes those versions had in common. I remember that Albert especially enjoyed how the crows played to Trickster's vanity by suggesting that the mysterious Hermit knew how to be alone better than Trickster himself did! I found it interesting that Trickster submits to the crow's magic—they turn *him* into a crow, whereas in most Trickster stories it is Trickster who shape-shifts on his own volition.

I also heard a story quite similar to "Trickster and the Best Hermit" at Flying Post, Ontario, an Ojibwa community.

Trickster and the Shut-Eye Dancers

In studies of comparative Algonquian folk literature—and in a small part evidenced by my own travels—the story of Trickster and the "shut-eye dance" is quite popular throughout the North. My rendition is based on three versions by Albert Sandy, and one by his cousin John Rains, all told near Family Lake, Manitoba. I also heard variations on the "shut-eye dance" theme at the Montagnais Indian community of Poste-de-la-Baleine, Quebec.

In "Trickster and the Shut-Eye Dancers," a reader can discover how Trickster goes to amazingly inventive lengths to dupe his utterly loyal sidekick, the fox. Once Fox discovers Trickster's betrayal, however, he turns into a storyteller: "After that, news of Trickster's betrayal traveled far and wide among foxes."

Trickster Tells Whiskey Jack the Truth

As noted in the introduction, my rendition of "Trickster Tells Whiskey Jack the Truth" is based on my work with Albert Sandy near Family Lake, Manitoba.

Trickster and the Walking Contest

"Trickster and the Walking Contest" was told by Job Walks, near Whitemud Lake, Manitoba. I worked with Job Walks on at least a dozen occasions over a five-year period, with as much as two years passing between visits. We also went over several subsequent versions in a hotel in Winnipeg, Manitoba, where Job had come to visit his brother in the hospital. I took a room in the same hotel and we worked on stories there. Job would visit his brother, eat most of his meals in the hospital cafeteria, then come back to the hotel. The final rendition of "Trickster and the Walking Contest" combines three of Job Walks's versions.

Trickster and the Clacking Sleeves

In three of the seven versions of "Trickster and the Clacking Sleeves" told to me over a three-year period by Joby Makinaw, near Bloodvein, Manitoba, Trickster begins his journey in four directions from Otter Lake. When I asked Joby Makinaw why, he answered, "It's where I first heard the story." Fundamentally, the only thing that changed rendition to rendition is what specific calamity befell Trickster in each direction. Among all seven versions, then, there accumulated an impressive array of ill fates. In one variation, for instance, while traveling south Trickster is ambushed by the "close-eye sleet." Later in the same tale, instead of seeing his own reflection on the surface of a lake, he sees the reflection of crows perched on a branch. The crows' laughter ripples the surface of the water.

In my rendition of "Trickster and the Clacking Sleeves," I combined calamities from two of Joby Makinaw's tellings.

Trickster and the Night-Tailed Weasels

I worked on "Trickster and the Night-Tailed Weasels" with Johnny Davis in Churchill, Manitoba, mostly in the Beluga Hotel, which sits beside the Churchill River where beluga whales come in to feed. In addition to "Trickster and the Night-Tailed Weasels," Johnny Davis told me two other stories about how Trickster had treated weasels, skunks, and squirrels badly, and how the animals got back at him.

Johnny Davis spoke English, Cree, some Inuit, and fluent French. The rendition of "Trickster and the Night-Tailed Weasels" in this book was completed through an exchange of letters. Mr. Davis died in 1989.

Trickster and the Fainting Birds

I first heard a version of "Trickster and the Fainting Birds" from Tommy Pike, in August of 1977, near Gods Lake, Manitoba. Some months later, he visited me in Ann Arbor, Michigan, where I was working on translations and writing film scripts about arctic and subarctic wildlife under the auspices of the University of Michigan's Society of Fellows. In Ann Arbor, we worked together on six stories; each of them involving one or another kind of contest between Trickster and human beings. But it was when I saw Tommy Pike actually tell a Trickster story in August of 1977 in his community, to an audience of perhaps twenty adults and children, that I first understood just how powerful, joyful, and uncanny a figure Trickster is in the North: That audience fell into sidesplitting laughter.

I recalled Albert Sandy saying, "Without Wistchahik, people might get lazy—lose their sense of humor!"

DATE DUE

GAYLORD